MONSTER!
HUNGRY!
PHONE!

For David Lloyd because he says,
"You don't need many words."
(Also because he used to be called
Mr Turkey Sandwich) – S.T.

To my little and big monsters:
Joachim, Salomé and Mattéo – F.B.

BLOOMSBURY CHILDREN'S BOOKS
Bloomsbury Publishing Plc
50 Bedford Square, London, WC1B 3DP, UK
29 Earlsfort Terrace, Dublin 2, Ireland

BLOOMSBURY, BLOOMSBURY CHILDREN'S BOOKS and the Diana logo are trademarks of Bloomsbury Publishing Plc
First published in Great Britain 2022 by Bloomsbury Publishing Plc

Text copyright © Sean Taylor 2022
Illustrations copyright © Fred Benaglia 2022

Sean Taylor and Fred Benaglia have asserted their rights under the Copyright, Designs and Patents Act, 1988,
to be identified as the Author and Illustrator of this work

A catalogue record for this book is available from the British Library

ISBN 978 1 5266 0678 5 (HB)
ISBN 978 1 5266 0680 8 (PB)
ISBN 978 1 5266 0679 2 (eBook)

1 3 5 7 9 10 8 6 4 2

Printed in China by Leo Paper Products, Heshan, Guangdong

MIX
Paper from
responsible sources
FSC® C020056
FSC
www.fsc.org

To find out more about our authors and books visit www.bloomsbury.com and sign up for our newsletters

MONSTER!
HUNGRY!
PHONE!

Easy Cheesy
PIZZA
deLivery

Sean Taylor

BLOOMSBURY
CHILDREN'S BOOKS
LONDON OXFORD NEW YORK NEW DELHI SYDNEY

Fred Benaglia

This is
a jaguar in
Nicaragua.

I'm Amanda the panda, playing ping-pong with a salamander.

This is the Voicemail of Simon Sloth. I'm sorry I'm probably asleep - if you'd like to leave a short message, please speak after the beeeeep!

WELL, I am sorry
but I can't help you.
I am an **ALIEN**
from **outer space** –
and you've caught
me right in the
middle of...

Oh my stars and golly gee! This is not the job for me!

MONSTER!
HUNGRY...